NICE LITTLE GIRLS

by Elizabeth Levy

illustrated by Mordicai Gerstein

Delacorte Press New York

Manufactured in the United States of America

SECOND PRINTING—1974

Library of Congress Cataloging in Publication Data

Levy, Elizabeth.
Nice little girls.

SUMMARY: Jackie has an adjustment problem at
her new school where everyone expects her to look
and act like "a nice little girl."
I.   Gerstein, Mordicai, illus.   II.   Title.
PZ7.L5827Ni   [E]   73-15394

ISBN: 0-440-06207-1 (tr)
0-440-06193-8 (lib)

When Jackie showed up at her new school, Mrs. James said, "This is the new boy in our class."

"I'm a girl!" said Jackie.

The whole class laughed.

"Oh, I'm so sorry," said Mrs. James. "Class don't laugh."

Later in the morning Mrs. James asked for someone to run the movie projector. Jackie raised her hand.

"Bill, will you help me?" asked Mrs. James.

Jackie put her hand down.

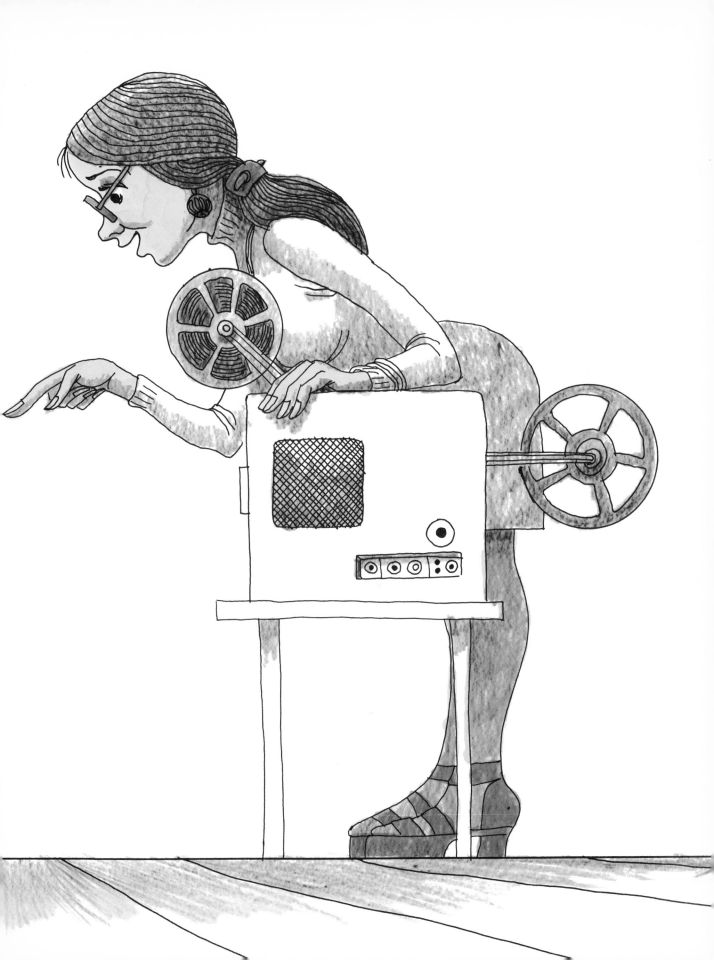

After lunch the class went to the playground.

"I bet you're not a girl," said Sam. "You don't look like one."

"I am too!" said Jackie, and she punched Sam in the arm.

"THE NEW GIRL'S A BOY...THE NEW GIRL'S A BOY!!" chanted Susie and Barbara, the two prettiest girls in the class.

Jackie told them to shut up.

Jackie hated being teased. She felt like crying, but she didn't want to be called a crybaby too. She looked at Susie and Barbara, who were so pretty.

All of a sudden she said to herself, "OK, if they want it that way, I'll be a boy. Anyhow, I can act like a boy."

"You're right," said Jackie. "I'm not a girl. I'm a boy."

"You're weird," said Barbara.

"I'm a boy! I'm a boy!" Jackie strutted up and down the playground.

The other kids joined in: "Jackie's a boy!! Jackie's a boy!!"

Jackie felt good for the first time that day. Everyone marched up and down.

Mrs. James came
running out.

"Please…" she
said. "You're making
too much noise."

Later that day Mrs. James asked,
"Who wants to build a box?"
Jackie raised her hand.
"Thank you, Jackie," said Mrs. James.
"But that's a boy's job."

"I can do it," Jackie blurted out. "I'm good at it. Besides I **am** a boy. You said so yourself."

"Jackie, dear," said Mrs. James, "it's time you started acting like a nice little girl."

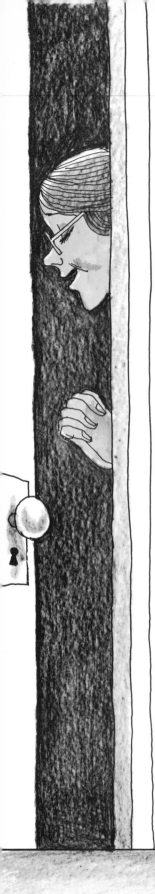

Jackie did not want to act like a "nice little girl"—not if it meant she couldn't build boxes. She needed some time to think, so she asked if she could be excused to go to the bathroom.

"Boys get to do all the good things," she muttered to herself.

Part way down the hall Jackie looked up and saw the door to the boys' room. Suddenly she felt like peeking in. Her heart was beating very fast. She knew she was doing something she shouldn't.

Uh, oh, Jackie thought when she got inside. What are **those** funny things? Jackie stared for a few seconds. Then she got very scared.

She ran to the girls' room as fast as she could.

"Everything's a mess!" she wailed. Jackie didn't know what to do.

She knew she couldn't really be a boy, but she wasn't going to be the kind of girl Mrs. James liked, either.

"Well," Jackie decided, "I can pretend to be a boy and do the things I want to do."

When Jackie walked back into class, Susie
looked up at her, but Jackie didn't notice.

All week Jackie tried to do whatever the boys did.

She lined up for boys' gym.

She tried to sneak into a Cub Scout meeting.

She didn't make any friends that first week.

At the end of the week Mrs. James called Jackie's mother. "I'm having a problem with Jackie," said Mrs. James. "She keeps acting like a boy."

Jackie was afraid she was in trouble.

Jackie's mother and father took her for a walk.

"Let's hear your side of the story," said Jackie's father.

Jackie told about her first day at school. "Everybody thought I was a boy, even the teacher. It was awful. So finally I said, OK, I'll be a boy. At first I meant it just as a joke. But I wish I **were** a boy. Mrs. James always gives girls the stupid jobs. She won't even let me build a box."

Jackie was having a hard time talking because she was trying not to cry. "I can't stand this new school," she said. "Susie and Barbara think I'm weird, and Mrs. James hates me. I know she does."

Jackie's father bent down and put his arms around her.

"Nobody hates you," he said. "Remember, it's always tough in a new school. I think you're a wonderful girl and I love you just the way you are."

"But Mrs. James doesn't," Jackie sniffled. "She called you 'cause I'm in trouble."

"Mrs. James just has silly ideas about what girls can and can't do," said Jackie's mother. "I'm proud that you know how to build a box."

"We'll talk to Mrs. James," said Jackie's father, "and tell her that there's nothing wrong with the things you want to do."

The next day Jackie went back to school.

"Your parents called," said Mrs. James. "They want to come in to see me. Did they talk to you about your problem?"

"Yes, they did," said Jackie.

"Are you going to be a nice little girl from now on?" asked Mrs. James.

"I **am** a girl!" said Jackie. "And I think it would be nice if you let me build a box."

Jackie went into a corner and started hammering.

After a while Susie came over and said, "Boy, you really told Mrs. James something."

"I'm not a boy!" said Jackie.

"Don't be so snooty," said Susie. "I didn't mean to call you a boy. I just think you're pretty brave, that's all."

"SUSIE!" yelled Barbara. "Since when do you play with boys? Come on over here."

"Go on," said Jackie. "You can't help me anyhow. I bet you don't know anything about building boxes."

Susie stayed where she was, and Barbara came over.

"Hey, Susie," said Barbara in a voice loud enough for Jackie to hear. "Let's decide who we're going to invite to your birthday party. It's just for girls, isn't it?"

"It's my party," said Susie. "I'll make my own list."

After school Jackie was walking home
alone.

"Hey, wait up," Susie called.

"What do you want?" asked Jackie.

"I don't like to walk alone," said
Susie. "Why don't we walk together?"

"OK," said Jackie.

When they got to Susie's house, Susie said, "Do you want to come in? I've got something special to show you."

"Sure," said Jackie.

Susie took Jackie up to the attic. "My secret room is up here," said Susie. "Come on in."

"Wow!" said Jackie.

They played with Susie's train set all afternoon.

When they got hungry, they went downstairs and Susie's mother gave them some cake.

"This is my friend Jackie," said Susie.

"I'm glad to meet you," said Susie's mother. "Susie has talked about you."

A couple of days later when Jackie
came home, there was a letter for her.

It was an invitation to Susie's birthday party.

The next day in school Jackie and Susie were painting when Barbara came up and whispered in Susie's ear "I want to talk to you about your party."

"We can talk about it in front of Jackie," said Susie. "She's coming."

"I thought this party was for girls," said Barbara. "I don't want to go to any party with boys."

"Jackie's not a boy," said Susie, waving her paintbrush in the air. "She's my friend. And if you don't want to come to my party, you don't have to."

"I want to go to your party," said Barbara.

"OK," said Susie. "You can go even though you are a boy." And she took her paintbrush and painted a big moustache on Barbara.

"Barbara's a boy!! Barbara's a boy!!"
said Jackie, jumping up and down.

"So are you," said Susie, painting a moustache on Jackie.

"You too," said Jackie, and she gave Susie a beautiful big moustache.

Soon everyone in the class was laughing and painting moustaches on each other. Even Mrs. James started to smile.

Then, before she knew what was happening,
Sam painted a big moustache on her.